My Great Grandma Clara

Written by Evelyn Rothstein

Illustrated by Elizabeth Uhlig

Marble House Editions

Published by Marble House Editions
96-09 66th Avenue (Suite 1D)
Rego Park, NY 11374

Library of Congress Cataloguing-in-Publication Data
Rothstein, Evelyn
My Great Grandma Clara/by Evelyn Rothstein

Summary: The tale of a young, Jewish woman who left her home
in Kobrin, Russia at the turn of the 20th century to make a new life
in the United States.

ISBN 0-9677047-8-2
Library of Congress Catalog Card Number 2005938648
Printed in China

This book is dedicated to my wonderful, loving grandchildren,

Tyler, Eliza, Abigail, Margo, and Jane.

Great Grandma Clara and Dad - 1958

My dad had two Grandmas. One was Great Grandma Clara, who was my Grandma Evelyn's mother.

I didn't know Clara, but my Grandma Evelyn always told me stories about her.

Grandma Evelyn and Me - 2005

Great Grandma Clara was born in 1903 in a small town in Russia called Kobrin, where her family had already lived for many years. The map shows where Kobrin is.

This is a very special map of what was once called *Jewish Eastern Europe*. Many of the places on this map have Yiddish, or Jewish, names.

Every dot • represents a town where Jewish people used to live. The Jewish people called their towns *shtetls*. Kobrin was one of these *shtetls*. Can you find it on the map?

This is what Kobrin might have looked like when Clara was a little girl.

This is the way my Great Grandma Clara told her story to my Grandma, who then told it to me.

I wasn't called Clara when I was born. My name was changed to Clara when I came to America. My mother and my father named me Hasha Etel, which was my Jewish name. When I was born, there were already three children in the family. After I was born, my mother would have three more children. This was the family.

Hannah   Leah   Lazar   Hasha Etel

Leibl   Shayndl   Golda

My family was very poor in Kobrin. All the children had jobs to do at home. My sisters, Hannah and Leah, helped my mother cook and clean. And everyone had to take a turn caring for Shayndl and Golda because they were still too little to take care of themselves.

Lazar and Leibl helped my father fix things inside and outside that were always getting broken. They also went to a school called a Heder, where they learned to read and write Hebrew. I was a little jealous because I also wanted to go to school.

But my sisters and I had to study in the house. And we didn't study Hebrew. Only the boys learned to read Hebrew. The girls learned to read Yiddish. That's the language we spoke at home and my mother could be our teacher.

I loved learning to read, but there was always so much else to do in the house. We only had one or two hours a day for reading.

But I did learn to cook! I loved helping my mother in the kitchen. I was only nine years old when my mother showed me how to make a delicious chicken soup for the Friday night Sabbath dinner. Then she taught me how to make matzoh balls for Passover and latkes for Chanukah. I would help my mother make blintzes and gefilte fish on days when the family did not eat meat.

I was almost 10 years old when Mama was about to have her eighth child. Of course, we were all excited. Papa called for the midwife, a woman in the village who helped deliver babies. We sat in the kitchen and waited to hear the cry of the new baby.

But something went wrong and the midwife didn't know what to do. Papa came into the kitchen, praying and crying. "Your Mama and the baby died," he sobbed.

My father and my sisters and brothers held on to each other and cried. We were very sad for a long, long time. I missed Mama so much and all of us had to work even harder to help Papa take care of the family.

Then more sadness came. When Mama died, Golda was only two years old. My sisters and I tried to take care of her, but Golda just cried and cried. "Please eat, Golda," I would beg. But she wouldn't eat and couldn't sleep. Nothing we did made her feel better.

"I want Mama," she cried. She got thinner and sadder and a few months later, Golda died. The rabbi came and told us that Golda had died of a broken heart.

With so much sadness, my sisters Hannah and Leah hoped to go to America. "Everyone says life in America is better," Hannah would say.

"If we can go to America we will get jobs and save money to send you," Leah would promise.

Then Hannah would add, "Maybe Mama's sister Rose will send for us. Aunt Rose went to New York a long time ago and maybe she has saved some money."

Then one day a letter came from Aunt Rose. It was written in Yiddish to my sisters, Hannah and Leah.

Dear Hannah and Leah,

I know how sad you all are because of Mama, and I know that life in Kobrin is not easy because there is so little work for anyone, especially girls. I have saved enough money for both of you to buy steamship tickets to America. I'm sorry that I can't send money for all of you, but when you are in America for one or two years, you can send for the family. I will be so happy to see you and talk with you about Mama and everyone else.

Aunt Rose

Hannah and Leah were both happy and sad. They were happy because they had heard from Aunt Rose and would be going to America. But they were sad because they would have to leave Papa and the rest of us. "We will send you money as soon as we can," promised Hannah. We all cried as we saw our family getting smaller and smaller.

אי"ן 6 צבר עולן כון לעיב

אלע מיין וואוי וו קארעסטאנדע 6/פר אוך צא'ן וואזן מוטער,
אי'ן אי'ק וויי'ן אס ראם אלע פטפמל אי'ן קומארין אלע שוועסר
ברי ועער אל/פ6, וא'ן, ג'ברד אל/ שוועטר בוד וו'ן לאפ6
בשוועיל, וויי'ב 6ס וו/ אלע 6ן ק6 ה'ן לאועראה".
אי'ק כ6ה רהב שו6בעבעם 6ל6אלעא אלא6 קעפ ווא רעיו"
שיעסקאפעם 16 אינדערעיעי. 66 6וס א'נ'ר וון, אלע
אי'ק קעלן קאפ6 שיקן קונען קארעלן אאר 6באר אל/6בי", וא6ר
וון אלע עס 6ן 13 ל"5 6על אלא6 אנרעדו ער6 6י'ן לאפ6ר אל6ר6
6/3 "ג', וועם אל'ר קעלן 6של6י"קע 6עס קעירן ה6יא

ג' ר6/6עם אא6ה6.

6ל6עם אא6ה6!

אי'ן 6עער אינ אאל 6עלן ר'אא6 6. אאאעה אל'ר 6. 6ל6עם 13
וון 6ל"5. 6י'ן עו 13 אוך א6ל6 6ל6עם 6ק'6עם 6ליקעם ק"6 6ל"5.

6ל6עם 57

Every day after Hannah and Leah left for America, I dreamed of getting a letter. But the letters they sent never got to Kobrin because a terrible war, World War I, broke out.

It was 1914. Germany invaded Russia and our little town of Kobrin was one of the towns Germany invaded. No mail could reach us now!

Hundreds of German soldiers came into Kobrin on horseback, and they carried big guns! Everyone in town was frightened.

Then one morning, two soldiers knocked on our door. I grabbed Shayndl and opened the door a crack. The soldiers kicked the door open and one shouted, "Where is your father?"

He didn't wait for an answer. The other soldier shouted, "We need your house. You will have to leave."

Just then, my father and two brothers came in from the shed where they were working. The two soldiers shouted back and forth.

"You and your family are to leave!"

"You are to be out of your house by this afternoon."

"Take only as much as you can carry and get out."

We started to pack, not knowing where we would go. Then suddenly the door opened again and another soldier walked in. Only this soldier was different. I knew he was an officer because of the hat he wore. I grabbed Shayndl again and started to shake.

Instead of shouting, though, the officer smiled. He spoke softly and slowly, so I almost understood everything he was saying.

"Your family can stay," he told us, "but you will all have to live in one room of the house. I am a doctor and I need the other rooms for my sick and wounded men. If you do as I say, we won't hurt you."

Imagine how relieved we were! Even all five of us staying in one room of our house was better than leaving and maybe living on the streets. I thanked the German doctor over and over again because even though he didn't belong in our house, he was as kind as he knew how to be.

The German doctor and his sick soldiers stayed in our house for two years. Life was harder than ever and many times we hardly had enough to eat. And even when we had food, there was no salt, and food without salt has no taste. Luckily, I had learned from Mama how to make food taste a little better without salt.

I remembered that Mama would say, "If you don't have salt, just use herring." Herring is a very salty fish because it comes from the ocean. So I would first cook the herring in water to make the water salty. Then I would put the chicken or meat into the salty water. The food tasted a little better, except to Shayndl who cried and said that everything tasted of herring. But what else could I do?

Then one day in 1917, the war ended and the German doctor and the sick soldiers left. We had our rooms back and hoped that life would get better.

But a few months after the Germans left, a new type of war broke out, a war called the Russian Revolution. Many Russian people were angry at their ruler, Czar Nicholas, and wanted a new government. There was fighting all over Russia, even in Kobrin.

Every day I would make a wish that we would get a letter from Hannah and Leah. It was now 1919 and I was giving up hope. But one day a letter came! A letter from Aunt Rose with money for us to leave Kobrin. I was dancing and spinning with happiness.

But just as I was so happy, I couldn't believe what I was hearing!
"I'm not going to America," Papa said.
"Why? Why?" I stamped my feet.
"I'm afraid."
"Afraid of what?" I shouted.
"I'm afraid that in America I will forget to be Jewish. Here in Kobrin I know what to do, how to pray, what to eat. I only know how to be Jewish in Kobrin."

Lazar and Leibl and Shayndl and I argued and fought. My father said "No! Kobrin is where I must live." We cried and begged. "No, no, never. I cannot go," he said.

Then one night, as we all sat crying, Papa told us that we could go without him. He would stay alone in Kobrin. He said that Lazar and Leibl should leave first, and Shayndl and I would go later. I think Papa hoped that I would change my mind and stay with him in Kobrin. But what would I do with my life in Kobrin, except be poor?

Lazar and Leibl left in 1919 and in the winter of 1920, I left Kobrin with Shayndl. I said goodbye to my father, knowing I might never see him again.

I was 17 years old and Shayndl was 12. We had to take a long trip from Kobrin to get to England, where the boat would take us to America.

Shayndl and I would travel for six months. Some other Jewish people from Kobrin were leaving, too. First, we all went by cart and horses to a city called Brest-Litovsk. There, we got on a train that took us to the city of Warsaw, in Poland.

Traveling was hard, but we also saw amazing things that we couldn't believe. In Warsaw, we had a day to walk around and for the first time, I saw buildings that were six floors high! "Look Shayndl," I shouted. "A building with six floors! Nothing in Kobrin was more than two floors." And Shayndl would hold on to me, almost afraid to look up.

From Warsaw, we took another train to Danzig, which was in Germany. All of us travelers were made to stay in a big hall without heat or beds. We slept on blankets and didn't even have pillows. Everyone would be examined by a nurse and anyone who was sick would be sent back to...I don't know where.

On the second night in this hall I got a high fever and I was worried that I had a serious sickness called typhoid. A nurse came around and told me to put a thermometer in my mouth. But when she wasn't looking, I took the thermometer out of my mouth and put it back just as she came around again. "You're normal," she muttered and let me pass. Shayndl was sick too, and could hardly eat. "You must eat Shayndl," I begged her. "Please eat, because I can't live without you."

From Danzig we went to Hamburg, also in Germany. As we got out of the train, I saw dozens of men in plaid skirts. Shayndl and I couldn't believe our eyes. "Why are men wearing such beautiful skirts?" we wondered. Then someone told us that these men were soldiers from a faraway place called Scotland. I kept staring at them even though I knew it wasn't polite.

After a few weeks in Hamburg, we got on another train and after many, many long hours, we were in Antwerp in the country of Belgium. In Antwerp we would take a ferry across the English Channel to England.

This map shows the long trip we had to take from Kobrin to England. The countries are written in black and the cities we passed through are written in red.

Aunt Rose had already written to cousins in England who met us at the ferry docks there. Imagine meeting cousins you never knew in England! They took us to London and for the first time, Shayndl and I heard people speaking English. Of course, we didn't understand a word. Luckily, they also spoke Yiddish.

We stayed with our cousins in England for a few weeks until it was time to get on the ship in Southampton that would take us to America.

I was excited and frightened. We would be on a big ocean liner for two weeks. We had third class tickets, which meant we were down in the bottom of the ship, but I didn't care. "In a little bit of time, Shayndl, we will be in America, in New York. We'll see Hannah and Leah and Lazar and Leibl. We're going to speak English, and you will go to school, Shayndl, and maybe all our wishes will come true."

Most of my wishes did come true. When I came to New York, Aunt Rose gave me a new name — Clara. She said that in America it was better to have a name that sounded "English, not Jewish," and she thought "Clara" was a pretty name. She also told Shayndl to call herself "Sylvia."

It was not hard for me to get a job in America. Because of Mama, I already knew how to sew, so soon I got a good job sewing in a factory. I was able to make beautiful clothes for myself and my sisters and even my new friends in America.

Hannah and Leah and Lazar and Leibl were happy to have their "little" sisters with them in America, so we were a family again. Except that Papa stayed in Kobrin. Of course, we never stopped missing Mama. I was glad to be in America because I knew that most of what I wished for could now happen.

And that is the story of my dad's grandma. Even though I never had a chance to meet my great grandmother, every time I hear her story, I feel that know her, at least a little bit.

Maybe someone in your family can tell you a story about one of your great grandmas or great grandpas.

About Kobrin: When Hasha Etel was born, Kobrin was a small town within Russia. It was very close to a region called Poland. At that time, though, Russia ruled over Kobrin.

After World War I, in 1920, Kobrin became part of Poland, which was a new country.

Kobrin remained part of Poland for many years. Then in 1939, Kobrin "changed" countries again. It became part of yet another new country called the Belorussian Soviet Socialist Republic.

In 1990, Kobrin "changed" again, when the Belorussian Soviet Socialist Republic became the country of Belarus.